To you, always.
To you, soon.

Dolores Brown

To my parents,
who taught me how to love.

Reza Dalvand

The Day of Your Arrival
Somos8 series

© Text: Dolores Brown, 2019
© Illustrations: Reza Dalvand, 2019
© Edition: NubeOcho, 2019
www.nubeocho.com · hello@nubeocho.com

Text editing: Rebecca Packard

Distributed in the United States by
Consortium Book Sales & Distribution

First edition: october 2019
ISBN: 978-84-17673-02-4
Legal deposit: M-39092-2018

Printed in Portugal.

THE DAY OF YOUR ARRIVAL

Dolores Brown   Reza Dalvand

nubeOCHO

Sometimes, when you want something so much,
you have the feeling that the wait is never-ending.

We had waited for you for so long.

We did not know when you would come.

We prepared your room
because we knew that one day you would be home.

We did not know what your name was,
or if your eyes were brown or blue.

Would you like cotton candy?
Or maybe hot chocolate?

Jack was also waiting for you.
A rabbit always makes winter warmer.

And Molly was waiting for you too.
A bath is always much more fun
with a floating duck.

One day, finally, you arrived.

We found out that
you indeed loved hot chocolate.
And cotton candy too.

But what you liked most was
cotton candy dipped in chocolate.

It was lovely getting to know
each other.

Little by little you met aunts and uncles,
cousins and lots of friends…

Sometimes we went to the mountains
to visit grandma and grandpa.

You remember Miss Rosy?
You loved being in her class.

After you arrived,
Jack and Molly were happier than ever.

And we were happy as can be.

We had waited a long time.
And finally, we were together.